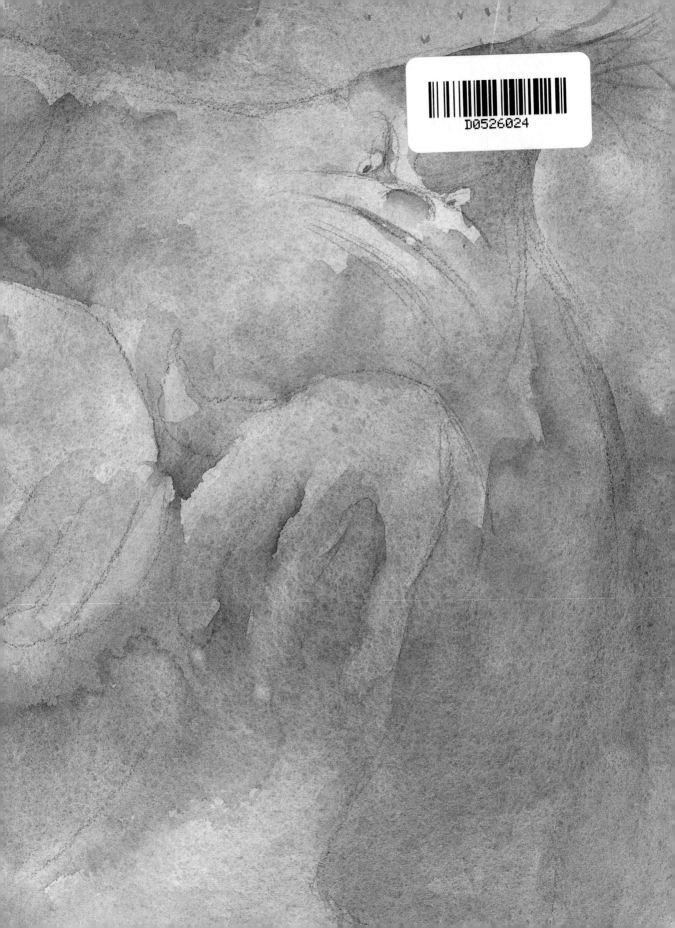

For Harry, Lily and Laura, with much love - L.C.
To June and Fred - P.U.

First published in Great Britain by Andersen Press Ltd in 1995
First published in Picture Lions in 1997
1 3 5 7 9 10 8 6 4 2
ISBN 0 00 664612 3
Picture Lions is an imprint of the Children's Division, part of
HarperCollins Publishers Ltd, 77-85 Fulham Palace Road,
Hammersmith, London W6 8JB.
Text copyright © Lindsay Camp 1995
Illustrations copyright © Peter Utton 1995
The author and illustrator assert the moral right to be identified as the
author and illustrator of the work.
Printed and bound in Hong Kong.

BILLY
AND THE BARGLEBOGLE

WRITTEN BY LINDSAY CAMP
ILLUSTRATED BY PETER UTTON

PictureLions

An Imprint of HarperCollins*Publishers*

WHEN BILLY'S MUM AND DAD brought the new baby home, nothing was the same in Billy's house.

Everything seemed upside down. There were flowers everywhere and the telephone kept ringing. Mum was very sleepy all the time. Dad wore his jeans, although it wasn't the weekend.

And people kept arriving to look at the baby and talk to it in funny voices.

Billy couldn't understand why everyone was so excited about it. He thought it was a funny colour, and its skin didn't seem to fit properly. And Dad said it wasn't big enough to ride on Billy's skateboard.

But the baby was only one of the things that was different
about Billy's house. The other was bigger. MUCH bigger!
It was the Barglebogle.
The first time Billy saw it was one evening, after his bath.
Mum was lying on the sofa. Billy asked her for his warm milk.

"Oh Billy, love," said his mum, "couldn't you just be a big boy and go and pour yourself some juice? I'm so exhausted I don't think I can move."

But there was no juice left in the box, and when Billy opened the fridge to look for some more, something whooshed out at him.

In seconds, the Barglebogle expanded until it almost filled the kitchen.

Billy stared up at the Barglebogle. The Barglebogle stared down at Billy. And before Billy could run away, it growled and wrapped its huge arms around him.

Billy was brave.

He bashed the Barglebogle. He butted the Barglebogle. But the Barglebogle was much stronger than Billy. He tried to shout for help, but the Barglebogle had one of its enormous paws over his mouth, and only grunting noises came out.

Then Billy bit the Barglebogle's paw as hard as he could.

The Barglebogle gave a huge roar—then suddenly disappeared, just as Billy's dad came rushing in.

"For goodness' sake, Billy, what's all the fuss about? The baby's just going to sleep!"

"It's nothing, Dad," said Billy, still trembling. "I just couldn't find any juice."

After that, Billy battled with the Barglebogle nearly every day.

Once, it jumped out on him when he was having a picnic in the garden with Mum and the baby.

Another time, it was waiting in the car when Billy came out of nursery school. And nearly every mealtime, it would be oozing around under the kitchen table.

Billy felt battered and bruised all over from fighting it off.

But there were two things about the Barglebogle that Billy didn't understand.

The first was why his parents hadn't noticed it. Billy thought it must be because they were so busy looking at the baby that they couldn't see anything else.

And the second thing Billy didn't understand about the Barglebogle was why it had come to live in his house. What was it after?

One day, Billy found out. His mum was making a long phone call. Billy was playing with his bricks. And the baby was lying on a quilt on the sofa.

Suddenly, the Barglebogle exploded out of the toy box. Billy got ready for another battle. But the Barglebogle pushed straight past Billy and snatched up the baby—

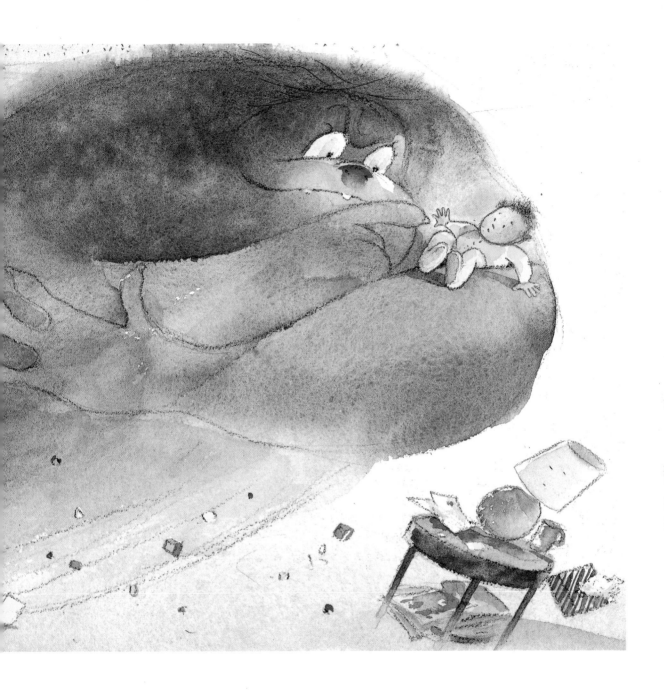

who started to howl and shriek.

Then, in a flash, Billy understood. The Barglebogle was after the baby! That was why it had arrived just after Mum and Dad had brought the baby home from the hospital. All the time, without even realising it, Billy had been protecting the baby from the Barglebogle!

The Barglebogle roared—and so did the baby, louder than ever. Its face was nearly purple.

The Barglebogle started lumbering towards the door. For a moment, Billy thought about letting it have the baby, so that everything could be the same as it used to be.

But only for a moment, because Billy wasn't a beastly boy. He strode up to the Barglebogle and said in a firm voice, "That's our baby. Give it to me right now, or I'll bite you even harder than last time!"

And the Barglebogle
was so surprised,
it did.

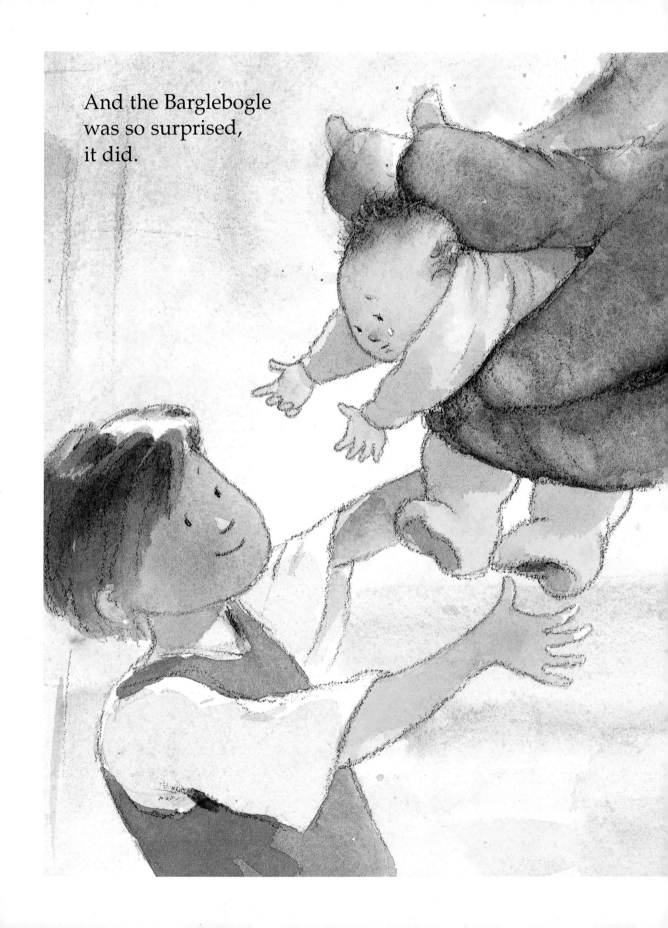

As soon as Billy took the baby in his arms, it stopped crying and looked up at him. Just then, Billy's mum came hurrying in to see what was the matter.

"Look, Mum," said Billy, "it's smiling at me! It really is smiling at me!"

"Of course she is," said Mum. "She loves being looked after by her smashing big brother."

And she gave Billy a big hug and a kiss.

What happened after that? Well, I'd like to tell you that Billy
never saw the Barglebogle again. But it wouldn't be true. It
did come back to Billy's house now and again. But somehow,
it didn't seem so frightening any more. It definitely wasn't as
big as it used to be, and its teeth and claws didn't look as
sharp.

Anyway, it didn't bother Billy because he knew that he could beat the Barglebogle if it ever tried to get the baby again.

And the baby must have known it too, because she was always smiling at her brave big brother.